I'm Tougher Than Diabetes!

Alden R. Carter

Photographs by ***Carol Shadis Carter***

Albert Whitman & Company • Morton Grove, Illinois

For the Aumann Family

Many thanks to all who helped with *I'm Tougher Than Diabetes!*, particularly Natalie, Kelsey, Laurie, and Dale Aumann; Clarence and Doris Aumann; Bernice and Lawrence Zywicki; Lynn Coleman, Linda Bubolz, and their students at Rudolph Elementary School, Rudolph, Wisconsin; Coaches Larry O'Shasky and Dave Dorhorst and their players; and Pam Alt, Kathy Ott, Betsy Suckow, and Lorraine Schafer, Ph.D., of the Marshfield Clinic, Marshfield, Wisconsin. As always, our children, Brian and Siri, and our editor, Abby Levine, have our special gratitude.

About the Author and Photographer

Alden R. Carter is the author of more than thirty books for children and young adults, including the celebrated novels *Up Country*, *Dogwolf*, *Between a Rock and a Hard Place*, and *Bull Catcher*. With his daughter, Siri, he wrote *I'm Tougher Than Asthma!*, an American Bookseller "Pick of the Lists."

Carol Shadis Carter is a social worker and a graduate of the Rocky Mountain School of Photography. Her work has appeared in several previous books by her husband, Alden, including *Big Brother Dustin* and *Dustin's Big School Day* (both with Dan Young), on Down syndrome; *Seeing Things My Way*, on visual impairment; and *Stretching Ourselves: Kids with Cerebral Palsy*.

Library of Congress Cataloging-in-Publication Data

Carter, Alden R.
I'm tougher than diabetes! / by Alden R. Carter ;
photographs by Carol Shadis Carter.
p. cm.
ISBN 0-8075-1572-8
1. Diabetes — Juvenile literature.
[1. Diabetes. 2. Diseases.]
I. Carter, Carol S., ill. II. Title.
RC660.5 .C67 2001
616.4'62 — dc21
2001000891

Text copyright © 2001 by Alden R. Carter.
Photographs copyright © 2001 by Carol Shadis Carter.
Published in 2001 by Albert Whitman & Company,
6340 Oakton Street, Morton Grove, Illinois 60053-2723.
Published simultaneously in Canada by
General Publishing, Limited, Toronto.
Printed in the United States.
10 9 8 7 6 5 4 3 2 1

The design is by Pamela Kende.
The text typeface is Caslon.

Note

Type I diabetes, like many chronic childhood illnesses, is a family affair. In *I'm Tougher Than Diabetes!* we see the healthy results when every family member has a positive and respected role in helping to manage diabetes.

I wish that were the case in all the families I see as a health psychologist. I wish, in fact, that it had been the case in my own family. I was diagnosed with Type I diabetes when I was nine. I don't recall being alarmed; my favorite grandmother had diabetes, and she seemed fine. Besides, I think I was feeling too awful to be upset. I didn't like the diagnostic testing in the hospital, but after a couple of days of treatment I felt pretty good.

But when I got home, things were different. My dad owned a construction company and worked long hours. His strength gave me confidence, but he never participated in my daily care, and that cost us an opportunity to grow closer. My brother was given no role in helping with my diabetes, and I now think that explained his occasional resentment; he felt left out. Mom and I worked to manage my diabetes, but after a time her constant concern started to suffocate me. I think she realized that, because the next summer she did something hugely courageous; she let me go off to 4-H camp on my own.

I loved camp. I learned to cook, speak in public, and square dance. I even had a romance. And I could do anything any other kid could as long as I took insulin and monitored the level of sugar in my blood. The kids accepted me for myself, noticing my diabetes only as a matter of passing interest. During all the up and down times I had after that, I always remembered that week.

I became a health psychologist because I am fascinated by how families react to illness and how they can learn positive strategies to help their ill members. In *I'm Tougher Than Diabetes!* we see a child with diabetes living with spunk, joy, courage, and confidence. Natalie, her parents, and her sister demonstrate how a family working together can not only learn to cope with diabetes but become a stronger and closer family in the process. Thank you, Natalie, for sharing your story. You are, indeed, tougher than diabetes!

Lorraine C. Schafer, Ph.D.
Health Psychologist

Hi, I'm Natalie, and this is Philomena, my diabetes kit. I have to take Philomena everywhere with me, which is kind of a pain. But the diabetes medicine she carries keeps me well, so I don't really mind.

Diabetes is a disorder people get when an organ called the pancreas (PAN-kree-uhs) doesn't work right. The pancreas produces a hormone (a body chemical) called insulin. Our bodies are powered by sugar from the foods we eat. Insulin helps the body's cells absorb that sugar.

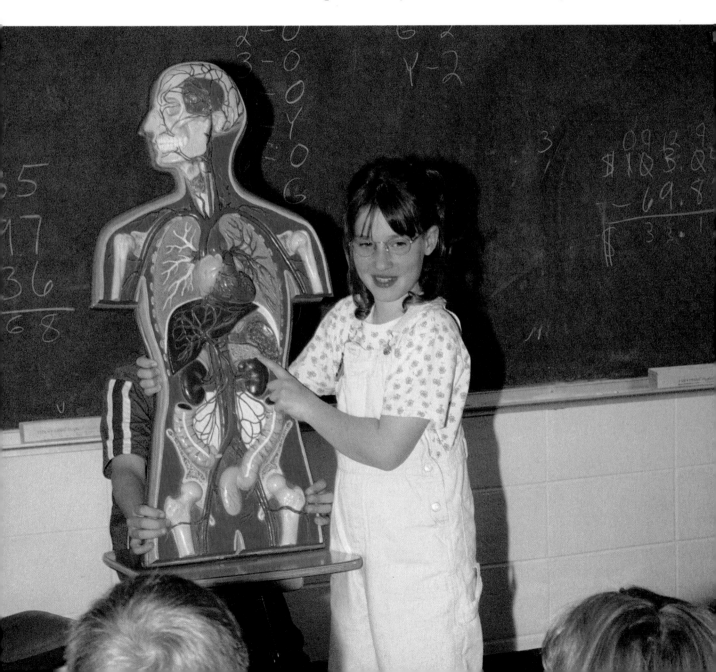

Because my pancreas doesn't produce enough insulin, extra sugar can build up in my blood. I keep my blood sugar at a healthy level by taking insulin shots at least twice a day. First I need to check how much sugar is in my blood. I do this by pricking my finger with a spring-loaded needle called a lancet. (It sounds awful but it's not too bad at all.) I put a drop of blood on a strip in my tester. For me, a reading of 80-140 is good. If I'm too low, I need a snack containing sugar. If I'm too high, I need more insulin.

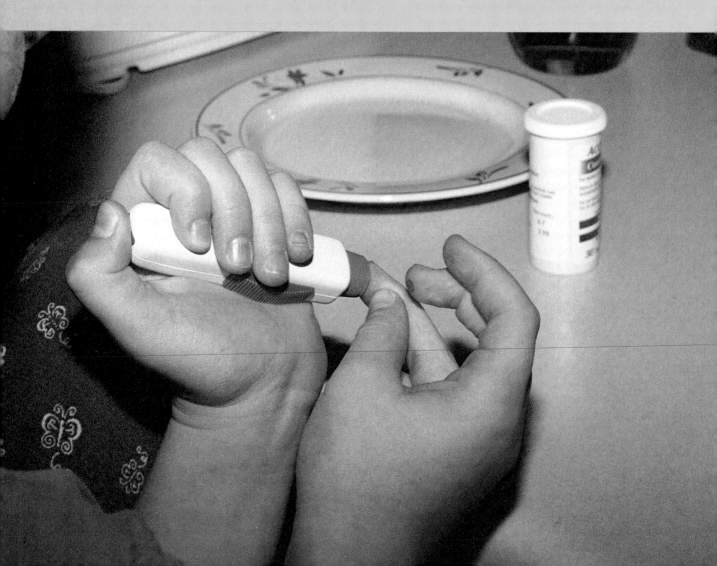

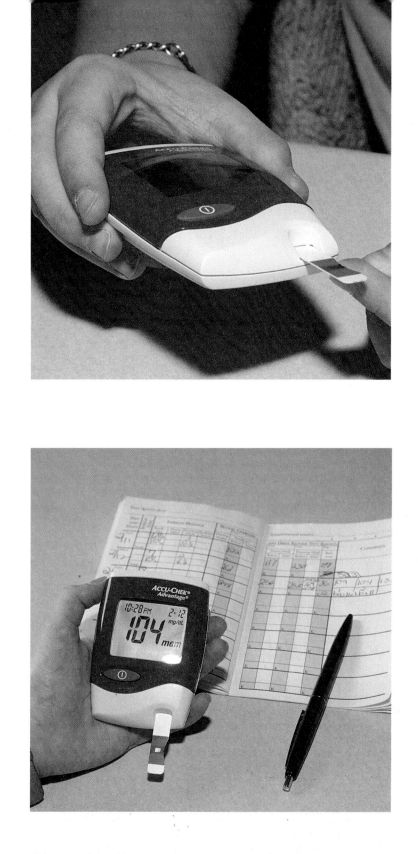

I'm learning to give myself shots, but I don't really like to do it all on my own yet. Mom and Dad say there's no rush, and one of them gives me my morning shot. The shots sting a little bit, but I got used to it a long time ago. And believe me, a little sting is a lot better than being sick.

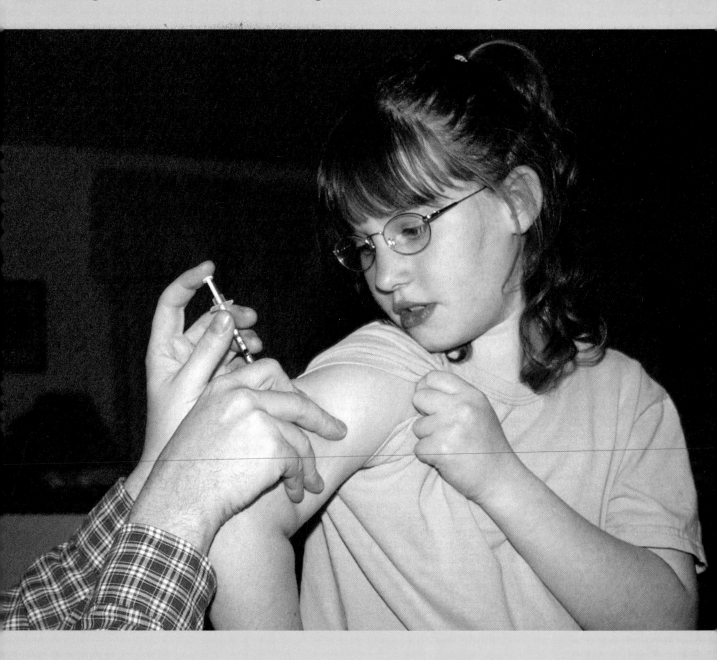

I keep a booklet to record my blood sugar readings, my shots, and my meals. To stay well, I have to really watch what and when I eat. I have three meals and five snacks every day. Mom says I'm a grazer, which means I eat more often than most people. (My sister, Kelsey, who wants to be a veterinarian, says it means I'm a cow, a goat, or a sheep.)

Mom and I spend a lot of time planning and making meals and snacks. I can have so many units of carbohydrates for each one. (Carbohydrates are the sugars and starches in plants.) A lot of people think that people with diabetes can't have sugar, but that's not true. We need sugar for energy, but we also need to balance the amount of sugar in our diet with the insulin we take. Carbohydrates are the best source of sugar for people with diabetes. Candy, cake, regular soda pop, syrup, and white and brown sugar are too sugary for us most of the time.

Mom and I weigh foods like carrots, potatoes, and apples to see how much I can have. We read the labels on boxes and look up different foods in the book the dietitian at the clinic gave us.

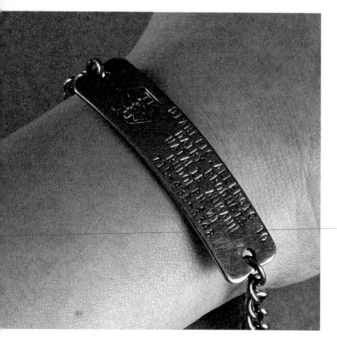

Kelsey and I go to Rudolph Elementary School. At the beginning of the year, Ms. Bubolz asked me if the class should have a rule against snacks made with sugar. But I said no, I don't want other kids to change for me.

My classmates are really great. I told them all about my diabetes and what I do to stay well. I showed them my ID bracelet and pictures of some famous people who have had diabetes: Thomas Edison, who invented the light bulb and about a million other things; the actors Elizabeth Taylor and Mary Tyler Moore; Nicole Johnson, Miss America 1999; and the Olympic gold-medal swimmer Gary Hall, Jr. But the part they liked best was when I showed them how I test my blood. They thought my tester was cool, and everybody cheered when I got a reading in my target range.

My diabetes started when I was six. At first Mom and Dad thought I had a virus. I felt so awful that Christmas that Kelsey had to help me open my presents! Mom and Dad took me to the doctor for some tests, and he put me in the hospital. It took a few days to get my blood sugar straightened out, but after that I felt a lot better.

Kelsey got mad when Mom and Dad didn't tell her everything right away. She said, "Natalie's my sister, and I'm going to help take care of her!" And she does. At Halloween this year she was especially sure to take all my candy. But I didn't mind. I had just as much fun as she did! (This year she was a princess, and I was a stop-and-go light.)

Exercise and staying in shape are especially important for people with diabetes. I like to swim and play tennis and basketball. Before I start to exercise hard, I have a snack to get my sugar up. Sometimes during a game I may check my blood again. If I'm low, I'll have a sugared drink or a piece of candy.

We're a really close family. And even if I don't like having diabetes (I mean, who would?), I'm glad we all work on it together. Someday, I'll have to handle diabetes on my own, but now I don't mind having a little help.

A couple of times a week, Dad and I check over Philomena. (Those nights I don't have to help with the dishes. Ha, ha.) Inside Philomena I carry my spare tester and lancet; extra test strips; insulin syringes; glucose (sugar) tablets; a list of emergency phone numbers; some change in case I need to call Mom or Dad; and what's called a glucagon emergency kit. (I'll tell you about that later. It's a little scary, but not too bad.)

Then we practice giving shots by injecting an orange about twenty times.

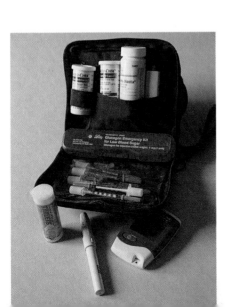

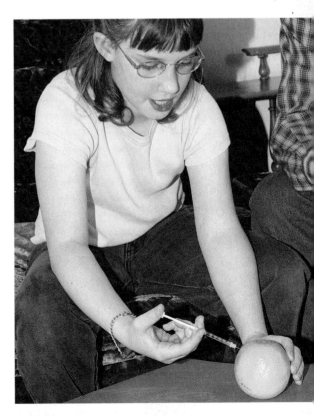

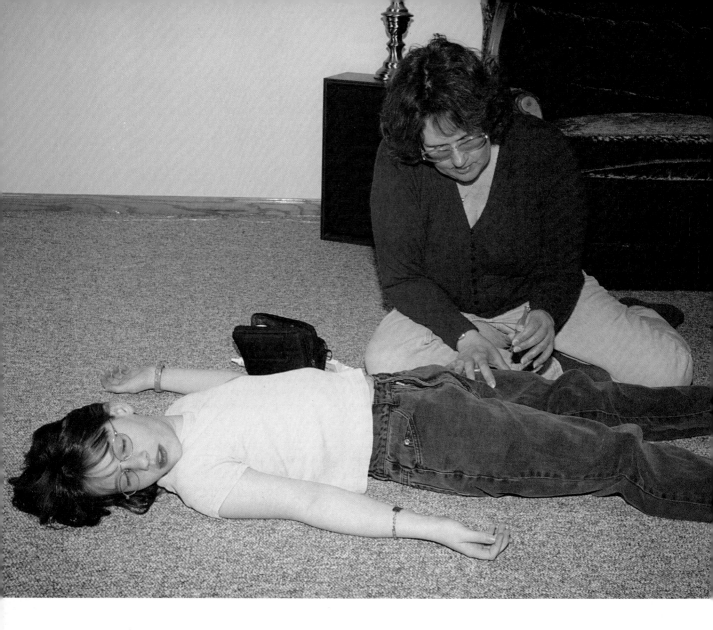

Next we all practice for an emergency. It's never happened to me, but if my blood sugar ever got really low, I could pass out. Then somebody will have to help me quick. (I always wear my bracelet that says I have diabetes.)

My emergency kit contains a syringe filled with glucagon, a hormone that will release all the sugar stored in my liver. The needle on the syringe is *really* long so it can go right through my clothing into my thigh.

When all that sugar hits my bloodstream I may throw up, so I'll need to be turned on my stomach so I don't choke. I'll wake up then, but I'll be real woozy and I'll need some help getting a sugar tablet in my mouth. I'll probably be OK in a few minutes, but I'll still need to be checked by a doctor.

Diabetes can be pretty goofy. If I get excited, like when Grandma and Grandpa are coming, my blood sugar may go high. Or if I play just a little extra hard, it may go real low.

I can usually tell when I'm high. I get hot, thirsty, kind of itchy and dizzy, and I need to go to the bathroom. I'll check my blood then, and if I'm really high I'll get a shot of insulin.

It's a lot harder to tell when I'm low. I may feel sweaty and headachy or I may just get tired and cranky. But what makes it really weird is how I don't think clearly. Last week we were playing croquet and I just kind of forgot about the game. Kelsey told Mom I was acting funny and that I might be low. Mom made me check my blood and my reading was all the way down to sixty!

When I'm low, I need to get some sugar in my system. It takes a while for my blood sugar to come back up. If it happens in the evening, Mom and Dad keep me awake, testing my blood every twenty minutes or so. And that's hard, because I'm tired and all I want to do is go to sleep. Finally, when my blood sugar is OK again, they take me to bed. Kelsey's always waiting up. She's like that.

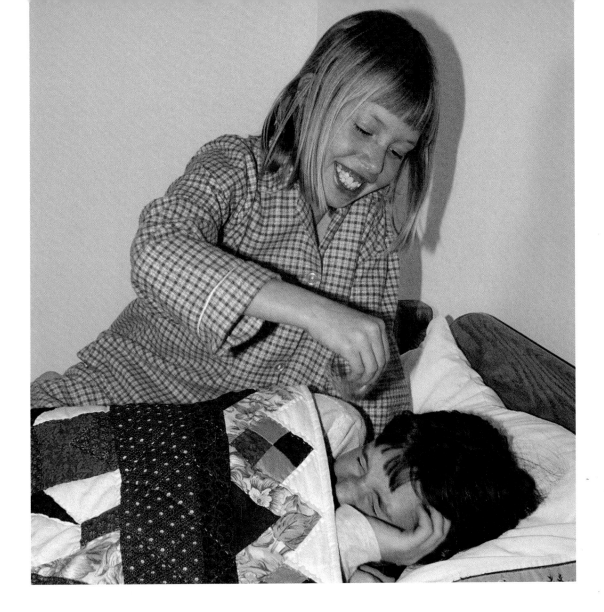

And the next thing I know Kelsey's tickling me and yelling and saying we're going to be late for school if I don't get my lazy bones out of bed. (She says all veterinarians have to be morning people.)

As soon as I've had breakfast, my morning blood test, and my shot, we're off to school. Kelsey says that someday we ought to be veterinarians together. But I'm going to be a librarian because I like reading better than anything, except maybe playing tennis. But no matter what I end up being, diabetes isn't going to stop me ...

*because I'm **tougher** than diabetes!*

Frequently Asked Questions about Diabetes

1. What is diabetes?

Diabetes is a disorder of the body's metabolism resulting from the failure of the pancreas to produce enough of the hormone insulin. Insulin enables cells to absorb sugars to power the body's functions. When the pancreas does not produce enough insulin, sugars build up in the bloodstream as the body's cells starve.

2. What are the types of diabetes?

Of the sixteen million people with diabetes in the United States, 90 to 95 percent have Type II diabetes. Type II diabetes usually occurs in people over forty and is usually controlled with diet and oral medications. Among children and adolescents, Type I diabetes is the most common form. It is typically controlled through diet, blood-glucose testing, exercise, and injections of insulin.

3. What are the symptoms of untreated Type I diabetes?

The body will try to rid itself of excess sugar through frequent urination. The untreated patient will seek to repair the resulting dehydration by drinking large quantities of liquids. Meanwhile, eating patterns are disrupted as the body's cells demand food in a vain attempt to get needed sugars. Some patients may overeat while others suffer a loss of appetite. In either case, patients will lose weight as the body begins to burn sugar stored in the liver and muscles.

The disturbance of the body's functions can cause various additional symptoms including crankiness, lethargy, fatigue, weakness, sadness, nausea, labored breathing, hot flashes, itchiness, and tingling in the extremities.

4. What is the initial treatment for Type I diabetes?

After the diagnosis of Type I diabetes, the patient will spend several days in the hospital or in an intensive outpatient program. During this time the patient undergoes testing to determine how much and what combination of short- and long-acting insulins suit his or her needs. A nurse educator will teach the patient and members of the family how to test blood sugar and inject insulin. A dietitian will meet with the patient and family to design a diet plan. A physical therapist may help with an exercise program.

5. *How often will the person with Type I diabetes need blood tests and insulin at home?*

Most people with Type I diabetes test their blood four or more times a day. Twice-daily injections of insulin are typical.

6. *Are the diets bland and unappealing?*

Not at all. Although high-sugar items will need to be avoided, the dietitian will help design a balanced diet plan that draws from all the major food groups, tastes good, and is healthy for nearly anyone to eat. A routine of eating the same amount at the same time daily will help to smooth out the peaks and dips in blood sugar.

7. *Why is an exercise plan important?*

Exercise helps control blood sugar and may reduce the amount of insulin needed. Exercise also decreases the risk of heart disease, lowers blood pressure, reduces stress, improves overall health, and gives a sense of well-being. Because even moderate exercise can reduce blood sugar to unsafe levels, the patient should begin slowly, advancing to more strenuous activities as he or she learns how to test and control blood sugar.

8. *What impact does stress have on blood sugar?*

People with diabetes need to test their blood frequently during times of stress. Stress will raise blood sugar for most people with diabetes, but young children in particular may experience a decrease in blood sugar.

The body deals with good and bad stress in much the same way. A child anticipating a holiday or overhearing a family fight may have an equal increase (or dip) in blood sugar. No one can avoid stress all the time. But many activities can help us control stress: communication with our families; exercise; hobbies; movies, television, and books; visiting a support group; or learning stress-management techniques.

9. *What are the symptoms of high and low blood sugar?*

Typical symptoms of high blood sugar (hyperglycemia) include: increased thirst and urination; high blood sugar readings; ketones in the urine (ketones are acids produced when the body burns sugar stored in the liver and muscles); weakness; aching; stomach pain; labored breathing; loss of appetite; nausea; vomiting; and fatigue. The usual solution is an additional dose of insulin. However, a patient or parent should not hesitate to consult a health professional.

Typical symptoms of low blood sugar (hypoglycemia) include: cold sweats; faintness and dizziness; headache; blurred vision; hunger; pounding heart; trembling; agitation; personality change (usually irritability); and sleepiness. Taking a simple sugar (glucose tablets, fruit juice, or a sugared soft drink) will usually resolve the problem. However, very low sugar may result in unconsciousness and the need for rapid emergency treatment. This may include the injection of the hormone glucagon to release sugar stored in the liver.

10. *How will a family react when a member is diagnosed with diabetes?*

All families are different, but typically the best results come when all family members are involved in supporting the person with diabetes. At first everyone may feel upset, sad, depressed, and irritable. But most families soon settle into a routine of blood testing, administering insulin, maintaining a healthy diet, and otherwise coping with diabetes. With the adjustment will come acceptance, confidence, and an improved sense of family cooperation. Many families enjoy the information, empathy, and activities available in local support groups.

11. *I've heard that teenagers often rebel against their programs for diabetes control.*

Teenagers with diabetes are no different from other teenagers in their need to test parental limits and their own capabilities. Many families experience additional stress as hormone changes upset previously successful routines for blood sugar management. However, families that have worked together usually find their young adults adjusting more quickly and with better spirits to the emotional and physical changes brought on by the teenage years.

12. *What do classmates and teachers need to know?*

A great many excellent educational materials are available to explain diabetes and its management. School staff who are educated about diabetes are more confident in helping the child with diabetes. Most schools train several staff members in how to give insulin injections. Often the child's older (or even younger) sibling assists.

The child's classmates need to be reassured that diabetes is not contagious and that they need not shy away from the friend they knew before. Actually, they may find that their friend is healthier and in better spirits than before his or her diabetes was diagnosed. Many children with diabetes gain confidence and win respect by showing and demonstrating their blood-testing equipment to the class.

13. *What future developments may help people with diabetes?*

Trials are underway on oral inhalers and nasal sprays to administer insulin. New devices are making blood testing faster, more accurate, and less troublesome. Soon most people with diabetes may wear watch-sized monitors that do not require the drawing of any blood at all. Insulin pumps to replace injections are becoming smaller, more sophisticated, and safer for younger ages. In coming years, monitors and pumps may be combined to provide continuous blood testing and insulin adjustment.

In very serious cases of diabetes, doctors can replace a malfunctioning pancreas with a healthy one. A promising procedure involves the implantation of insulin-producing islet cells from a healthy pancreas. Both procedures require powerful anti-rejection drugs with serious side effects, but new drugs and new methods of harvesting cells may one day make islet-cell implantation commonplace.

Ongoing research holds the real hope for a cure for diabetes. Eventually, we may have a means of preventing diabetes altogether. But in the meantime the vast majority of people with Type I diabetes can live full and happy lives through diabetes management and the support of loved ones.

Resources

American Diabetes Association
1701 North Beauregard Street
Alexandria, VA 22311
1-800-DIABETES
http://www.diabetes.org

Canadian Diabetes Association
15 Toronto Street, Suite 800
Toronto, ON M5C 2E3
1-800-BANTING
http://www.diabetes.ca

Children with Diabetes Foundation
2525 Arapahoe, Suite E4
PMB 506
Boulder, CO 80302
http://www.cwdfoundation.org

Diabetes Research and Wellness Foundation
1206 Potomac Street
Washington, DC 20007
http://www.diabeteswellness.net
Offers free diabetes identification jewelry

Juvenile Diabetes Foundation International
120 Wall St., 19th Floor
New York, NY 10005-4001
1-800-533-2873
http://www.jdf.org

Sugarbugs, Inc.
2354 Highway 41, Ste. J
Greenbrier, Tennessee 37073
toll free: 1-888-699-2847
http://www.sugarbugs.org
Especially for kids